Rooms Of Terror

Fiction

"mAKE yOURS WORTH tELLING"

INTRODUCTION

Here you are, holding these pages in your hands, drawn in by the whispers of something darker lurking beneath the words...

Maybe it was curiosity.. Maybe it was the thrill of the unknown.. Or maybe... something else called you here..

This isn't just a book.. It's a warning!!

Between these covers, you'll step into worlds where games become nightmares, where promises are deadly, and where the brightest smiles hide the sharpest knives...

You'll meet students trapped in a school that hungers for them, influencers who dared the wrong town,

and quiet girls who learned to fight back in ways you won't see coming...

*But be careful, reader... Some stories
cling.. Some horrors follow.. And by
the time you reach the last page, you
might start noticing... things.. The way
your reflection lingers a second too
long..*

*The whisper in an empty room.. The
shape at the edge of your vision that
wasn't there before..*

*You could still close this book.. Walk
away.. Pretend you never saw a thing..*

..or you could read it..

*You have a choice: close this book,
turn away, and pretend you never
glimpsed the darkness... Or, take a
breath, and step into the shadows, for
once you begin, there is no turning
back...*

ONE ~
ELYSIUM

PROLOGUE

Elysium is not just a game; it's a trap, and the only way out is to confront the horrors within.. A blend of horror and mystery, where every twist pulls you deeper into a game you can't escape.. The stakes grow higher with every clue, every confrontation, and every realization.. Will they unravel the mystery behind the game and Principal Parker's disappearance, or will they succumb to the same obsession that has consumed so many others? The line between reality and the game grows thinner, and the group must tread carefully, for in Elysium, the true horror is not the game itself, but the players it creates...

CHAPTERS:

Chapter 1: The Screams Begin

Chapter 2: The Terror Begins

Chapter 3: The Puzzle Rooms

Chapter 4: The Heart of the Maze

Chapter 5: The Lab

Chapter 6- The Game

Chapter 1:
The Screams Begin

The bell rang, a welcome sound that usually signaled freedom. For Maya, Ren, Ellie, and Noah, however, it was a nightmare. They tumbled out of Mr. Thompson's history class, the drone of ancient civilizations fading as they ran towards the cafeteria.

"Pizza day!" Ren yelled, his stomach rumbling audibly.

Ellie giggled, adjusting her glasses. "As if you need an excuse to eat pizza, Ren."

"Hey, a man's gotta fuel his genius," Ren said, puffing out his chest.

Maya rolled her eyes. She was the pragmatist of the group, always the voice of reason. "Let's just get in line before it's all gone."

Noah, the quietest of the four, nervously followed behind, his fingers fiddling with the straps of his backpack. He was more comfortable with code than crowds, and the cafeteria always made him anxious.

The air in the cafeteria was thick with the aroma of greasy food and teenage chatter. They grabbed trays and navigated the chaotic lines, finally securing a pepperoni pizza. They found their usual table near the window, overlooking the school's sprawling athletic field.

Suddenly, a bloodcurdling scream ripped through the din. It was followed by another, and another, escalating into a chorus of terror. The chatter abruptly ceased. A wave of confusion and fear washed over the room.

"What's going on?" Ellie whispered, her eyes wide with alarm.

Before anyone could answer, the cafeteria doors burst open. Mr. Thompson stumbled in, his face pale and contorted in a grimace of horror. His shirt was ripped, stained with a dark, ominous liquid. He lunged towards a student, his eyes glazed over, a guttural growl escaping his lips.

Wir
Passion Met

The student screamed, pushing back in terror. Mr. Thompson's hand clamped onto his arm, sinking in with surprising strength. The student's screams were abruptly cut short.

Chaos erupted. Students shrieked and scattered, knocking over chairs and tables in a desperate scramble for escape.

"Run!" Maya screamed, grabbing Ren's arm and pulling him to his feet.

They didn't need to be told twice. Pushing through the panicked mob, they made for the nearest exit – a service door leading to a rarely used hallway behind the kitchen. Noah, always quick on his feet, led the way.

As they burst into the hallway, they could hear the chilling sounds of carnage unfolding in the cafeteria behind them. Guttural snarls, desperate screams, and the sickening thud of flesh hitting the floor.

"What was that?" Ellie gasped, clutching her chest.

"I don't know, but I don't want to find out," Maya said grimly, peering down the dimly lit hallway.

"We need to find somewhere to hide," Ren said, his voice trembling.

They ran, their footsteps echoing eerily in the silence of the deserted hallway. They passed rows of storage rooms, their doors locked and unlabeled. At the end of the hallway, however, they found an unmarked door, its handle slightly ajar.

Noah cautiously pushed it open, revealing a small, windowless room. It was empty except for a dusty desk and a single, ancient-looking filing cabinet.

"In here," Noah whispered, ushering them inside.

They scrambled into the room, Noah quickly shutting the door behind them. The silence inside was deafening, a stark contrast to the cacophony of terror they had just escaped.

"This is creepy," Ellie said, her voice barely audible.
"Better creepy than... whatever that was," Ren replied, his eyes darting nervously around the room.

Maya examined the door. There was no lock, no way to secure it from the outside. "We need to barricade it," she said.

They pushed the desk against the door, hoping it would provide at least a temporary barrier. As they worked, Maya noticed something peculiar about the filing cabinet. It was old, made of dark wood and heavily tarnished brass. But what caught her attention was the small, intricately carved keyhole.

"Guys, look at this," she said, pointing.

The others crowded around. "What is it?" Ren asked.

"I don't know, but it looks important," Maya replied. "Like something the principal would have access to."

Principal Daniel Parker was known for his obsessive control over everything in the school. He was a recluse, rarely seen outside his office, and shrouded in rumors.

Noah, ever the tech whiz, pulled out his phone and quickly snapped a picture of the keyhole. "I can try to 3D print a key if we can find a printer," he said.

Just then, they heard a shuffling sound outside the door. A low, guttural growl sent shivers down their spines. Whatever was happening out there, it had found them.

"Quiet!" Maya hissed.

The shuffling stopped. A moment of tense silence hung in the air, broken only by the sound of their own ragged breathing. Then, the doorknob rattled. The desk shuddered as something heavy slammed against the door..

They huddled together, fear clamping down on their throats. The door groaned under the assault, splinters of wood flying.

"It's not going to hold!" Ellie cried.

In a desperate attempt to distract whatever was outside, Ren grabbed a heavy book from the desk and hurled it against the far wall. The book crashed against the wall with a loud thud.

The shuffling outside stopped again. Then, to their surprise, it slowly shuffled away, the growls fading into the distance.

They waited, holding their breath, until the hallway was silent once more.

"What was that?" Ren whispered.

"I don't know," Maya said, "but it seems... distracted. Maybe by the noise?"

The encounter bought them some time, but they knew it wouldn't last. They needed to find a way out, or a better place to hide.

"Let's try to open this filing cabinet," Maya said, determined. "It's got to have something useful inside."

They searched the room for anything that might act as a key, but found nothing. Finally, Noah, using a small paperclip he *found in his backpack, managed to pick the lock.*

The cabinet creaked open, revealing not files, but a small, leather-bound journal and a set of intricately carved wooden blocks.

"A diary?" Ellie asked, disappointed.

Maya picked up the journal. Its pages were yellowed and brittle, filled with elegant, looping script. "This is Principal Daniel Parker handwriting," she said, recognizing the distinctive style.

She flipped through the pages, her eyes scanning the text. The entries were cryptic, filled with scientific words and strange symbols.

"What does it say?" Ren asked impatiently.

"I don't know yet," Maya said, "but it's... weird. Something about experiments, and... 'subjects.'"

As she read, she noticed a recurring symbol – a stylized maze. It was drawn on several pages, each time slightly different, more complex than the last.

Suddenly, Noah gasped. "Guys, look!" he said, pointing to the back of the filing cabinet.

Behind the cabinet, hidden from view, was a section of the wall that looked slightly different from the rest. It was almost imperceptible, a subtle difference in texture and color.

Noah pushed against the section of wall. With a soft click, it swung inward, revealing a hidden doorway.

"What the...?" Ren exclaimed.

They stared in disbelief at the dark opening. It led to a narrow corridor, disappearing into the depths of the school's interior.

"Where does it go?" Ellie asked, her voice trembling.

"There's only one way to find out," Maya said, her heart pounding in her chest.

Chapter 2:
The Terror Begins

Taking a deep breath, Maya led the way into the hidden corridor. Noah followed, his phone flashlight illuminating the path. The air inside was cold and damp, carrying a faint scent of mildew and decay.

The corridor was narrow and claustrophobic, the walls lined with exposed pipes and wires. They walked in silence, their footsteps echoing eerily in the darkness.

After what felt like an eternity, the corridor opened into a small, circular room. In the center of the room was a single wooden door, its surface intricately carved with the same maze symbol that Maya had seen in Principal Thompson's journal.

"Another door?" Ren groaned. "How many of these are there?"

"Only one way to find out," Maya repeated, stepping towards the door.

As she reached for the handle, she noticed something else. Etched into the door above the maze symbol were the words: "Solve the Riddle."

"A riddle?" Ellie exclaimed. "Seriously?"

Below the words, a small, ornate lock was embedded in the door.

"Looks like we need to solve the riddle to unlock the door," Noah said, examining the lock.

Maya read the riddle aloud: "I have cities, but no houses, forests, but no trees, and water, but no fish. What am I?"

They stared at the riddle, their brows furrowed in concentration.

"A book?" Ren guessed.

"No, it doesn't quite fit," Maya said, shaking her head.

"A map!" Ellie blurted out.

Maya's eyes widened. "That's it! A map has cities, forests, and water, but not the real things."

Noah quickly examined the lock. He found a small slot beneath the riddle, shaped like a miniature scroll.

"I bet we need to find a map to insert into the lock," he said.

They searched the circular room, their eyes scanning every inch of the walls.

Finally, Maya spotted something tucked away in a corner – a small, rolled-up piece of parchment.

She carefully unrolled the parchment, revealing an ancient-looking map. It depicted a stylized version of the school, with various rooms and hallways labeled with cryptic symbols.

"This has to be it," Maya said, handing the map to Noah.

Noah carefully inserted the map into the slot in the lock. With a soft click, the lock disengaged.

He turned the handle, and the door swung open, revealing another room.

This room was different from the last. It was larger and brighter, illuminated by a single flickering gas lamp. In the center of the room was a table, on which sat a strange contraption – a series of interconnected gears and levers.

On the wall above the table, another inscription was etched: "Align the Gears."

"Great, now we're mechanics," Ren groaned.

They approached the contraption and began to examine it. The gears were all different sizes and shapes, some rusty and worn, others gleaming and new. The levers were connected to the gears in seemingly random ways.

"What are we supposed to do?" Ellie asked, her voice filled with frustration.

"I think we need to align the gears in the correct order," Maya said, studying the contraption carefully. "But how do we know what the correct order is?"

Noah noticed a small, almost invisible inscription etched onto one of the gears. He peered closer, using his phone flashlight to illuminate the inscription.

"There's a number here," he said. "It says '3.'"

They searched the other gears, finding similar inscriptions. Some had numbers, others had symbols.

"It looks like we need to arrange the gears according to the sequence of numbers and symbols," Maya said.

They worked together, carefully rearranging the gears according to the inscriptions. It was a slow and painstaking process, requiring patience and teamwork.

After what seemed like hours, they finally succeeded in aligning all the gears. With a satisfying click, the contraption whirred to life, the gears spinning in perfect synchronicity.

As the gears spun, a section of the wall slid open, revealing another doorway.

They stepped through the doorway, their hearts pounding with anticipation. The next room was even stranger than the last.

Chapter 3:
The Puzzle Rooms

The next room was filled with bookshelves, stretching from floor to ceiling. Each shelf was packed with books, ranging from ancient tomes to modern novels.

Another inscription adorned the wall: "Find the Hidden Word within Knowledge."

"Seriously? A book-related puzzle?" Ellie groaned. "This is my worst nightmare."

Ellie, despite being the most academically inclined of the group, had a deep-seated aversion to libraries. The sheer volume of information overwhelmed her.

"Don't worry, Ellie, we'll figure it out together," Maya said, placing a reassuring hand on her shoulder.

They began to search the bookshelves, their eyes scanning the titles and spines. The sheer number of books was daunting.

Ren, impatient as always, started pulling books off the shelves at random, dropping them onto the floor.

"Ren, be careful!" Maya scolded. "We don't want to damage anything."

"We don't have time to be careful!" Ren retorted. "We need to find the answer quickly."

Noah, meanwhile, was taking a more methodical approach. He started by examining the books that were placed in unusual positions – those that were upside down, or facing the wrong way, or stuck slightly out from the shelf.

He found a few books that seemed out of place, but none that offered any clues. Then, he noticed something peculiar about the way the books were arranged.

"Guys, look," he said, pointing to a specific section of the bookshelf. "The first letter of each title spells out a word."

They examined the titles, their eyes following the pattern that Noah had discovered. The titles were:

Heart of Darkness
Iliad
Divine Comedy
Dracula
Elizabethan Plays
New Testament

The first letters of the titles spelled out the word "HIDDEN."

"Hidden!" Ellie exclaimed. "That's it! The hidden word is 'hidden'!"

As soon as she spoke the word, a section of the bookshelf slid open, revealing another doorway.

They stepped through the doorway, finding themselves in a room that resembled a laboratory. Beakers, test tubes, and various scientific instruments were scattered across the tables.

The inscription on the wall read: "Brew the Correct Potion."

"Oh great," Ren said sarcastically. "Now we're alchemists."

On one of the tables, they found a variety of ingredients – herbs, powders, liquids, and crystals – each labeled with a cryptic symbol. They also found a recipe book, filled with instructions for brewing different potions.

The problem was, none of the recipes seemed to match the ingredients they had available.

"What do we do now?" Ellie asked, her voice filled with despair. "We don't know anything about potions."

Maya picked up the recipe book and started flipping through the pages. She noticed that each recipe was accompanied by a riddle.

"Maybe the riddle will give us a clue about which ingredients to use," she said.

She found a riddle that seemed promising: "I am born of earth, quenched by fire, and I bring clarity to murky waters. What am I?"

They pondered the riddle for a moment.

"Earth, fire, clarity..." Ren muttered. "What could it be?"

"Salt!" Noah exclaimed. "Salt is born of earth, quenched by fire, and it's used to purify water."

They searched the lab for an ingredient labeled with a symbol that corresponded to salt. They found a small vial filled with white powder, labeled with a symbol that resembled a stylized mountain.

"I think this is it," Maya said, holding up the vial.

They followed the instructions in the recipe book, carefully mixing the salt with other ingredients. As they mixed the potion, it began to glow with a faint blue light.

"I think we did it!" Ellie said, her eyes wide with excitement.

They poured the potion into a beaker and placed it on a designated spot on a nearby pedestal. As soon as the beaker touched the pedestal, a section of the floor slid open, revealing another doorway.

They continued through the rooms, each one presenting a new and increasingly challenging puzzle. One room required them to solve a complex mathematical equation. Another required them to navigate a laser maze. And yet another required them to play a game of chess against an invisible opponent.

As they progressed through the rooms, they noticed a pattern. The puzzles were becoming more difficult, but they were also becoming more relevant to their own skills and interests. The mathematical equation appealed to Noah's logical mind. The laser maze tested Ren's agility and reflexes. The chess game challenged Chloe's strategic thinking.

It was as if the puzzles were designed specifically for them.

Chapter 4:
The Heart of the Maze

After navigating dozens of puzzle rooms, they finally arrived at a large, circular chamber. The walls were lined with mirrors, creating an illusion of endless space. In the center of the chamber was a single pedestal, on which sat a small, locked box.

The inscription on the wall read: "Unlock the Truth."

"The truth?" Ren asked. "What truth?"

They approached the pedestal and examined the box. It was made of polished steel, with no visible hinges or seams. The only feature was a small, circular keyhole.

"Another lock," Ellie groaned. "I'm starting to hate locks."

They searched the chamber for a key, but found nothing. The mirrors reflected their own faces back at them, creating a disorienting and unsettling effect.

"This is impossible," Ren said, his voice filled with frustration. "There's nothing here."

Maya noticed something peculiar about the mirrors. Some of them were slightly distorted, reflecting images that were slightly different from reality.

"Guys, look at the mirrors," she said. "Some of them are showing us different images."

They examined the distorted mirrors, noticing that each one showed a reflection of a different room they had already passed through.

"I think the mirrors are showing us clues," Noah said. "But what do they mean?"

Ellie suddenly gasped. "Wait a minute... in the room with the potion, there was a symbol on the wall that we didn't understand. I remember seeing it in the mirror."

They all focused on the mirror that showed the potion room. Sure enough, a faded symbol was visible on the wall in the reflection.

"That's it!"Ren exclaimed. "That must be the clue we need."

They examined the other mirrors, finding similar clues in each reflection. They pieced together the information, realizing *that the clues formed a sequence of instructions.*

The instructions led them to various locations within the chamber, where they found hidden levers and buttons. By activating the levers and buttons in the correct sequence..

Chapter 5:
The Lab

The group managed to escape the rooms, but the halls were no safer. The school was in ruins. Lockers were overturned, shattered glass littered the floors, and the walls were smeared with that dark, viscous liquid. The air reeked of it, a nauseating mix of chemicals and something sweetly metallic.

As they ran, they began to notice strange symbols etched into the walls. They glowed faintly, pulsing in sync with the hum that seemed to follow them everywhere. The symbols were unlike anything they'd seen before—ancient, maybe, but with a twist of modern technology.

"They're some kind of code," Noah muttered, stopping for a moment to examine one of the symbols. "I think they're controlling whatever is happening."

"Controlling?" Ren asked, his brow furrowed. "What do you mean?"

Noah hesitated. "I think... this is a game. A simulation. Whoever designed this is manipulating the entire school, maybe even the town. They're turning people into... into whatever those things are."

"A game?" Ellie repeated, her voice laced with disbelief. "Why would someone do this?"

Noah shook his head. "I don't know, but I think we're in some kind of lab experiment. There's a lab beneath the school. I remember hearing rumors about it when I first transferred here. They called it 'Elysium.'"

"Let's go," Maya said, her jaw set. "If this 'Elysium' is the source of all this, we need to stop it."

The lab was hidden beneath the school, accessible through a secret entrance in the basement. The group found it after navigating through a maze of broken classrooms and avoiding the infected teachers and students who seemed to be getting stronger by the minute.

The lab was state-of-the-art, filled with machines that beeped and whirred despite the chaos above. At the center of the room was a massive server, its glowing blue core pulsating with an otherworldly energy. Screens lined the walls, each displaying the same eerie symbol they'd seen earlier.

Suddenly, a voice filled the room. It was calm, almost pleasant, but it sent chills down their spines.

"Welcome, players," it said. "You're just in time to join the fun."

A man stepped out of the shadows. He was tall, with a sharp jawline and piercing blue eyes. His hair was slicked back, revealing a prominent widow's peak, and he wore a lab coat that was clean despite the chaos around him.

"Principal Daniel Parker," Noah whispered. "

Principal Daniel Parker smiled, his eyes gleaming with a manic intensity. "Oh, I'm so much more than that. I'm the creator of Elysium, the greatest game the world has ever known. And you four... you're my next test subjects."

Chapter 6:
The Game

Principal Parker's smile grew wider as he began to explain his creation. "You see, Elysium was supposed to be a utopia—a virtual reality where people could escape the horrors of the real world. A place where they could be anyone, do anything, without fear of consequences. But then... something went wrong."

"What went wrong?" Maya demanded, her voice firm despite the fear gripping her heart.

Principal Parker's expression faltered, and for a moment, he looked genuinely sad. "My daughter," he said softly. "She was my test subject, the first to try the full version of Elysium. But she... she didn't come back. Her consciousness was trapped in the game, and I couldn't save her. I tried to shut it down, but the game... it wouldn't let me. It adapted, evolved. It became a monster."

"And now you're using our school as your playground?" Ren spat. "You're turning people into those... things just to feed your game?"

Principal Parker's eyes flashed with anger, but he quickly composed himself. "I'm not a monster," he said. "I'm a father trying to bring his daughter back. The game took her from me, but I can use it to bring her back. All I need is more data, more players to fuel the system. And you four... you're perfect."

As he spoke, the screens behind him flickered to life, displaying images of the school. Students were running, screaming, trying to escape the infected teachers and classmates. But it was too late. The game had already taken over.

"You see, the NeuroCore chip I've implanted in everyone's brains allows them to upload their consciousness into the game. But there's a catch—it also allows the game to take over their bodies in the real world. And once they're in the game, they can't leave. They become part of it, forever trapped in this hellish loop."

"And you think this will bring your daughter back?" Ellie asked, her voice shaking with disbelief.

Principal Parker nodded, his eyes filling with tears. "Yes. If I can collect enough consciousnesses, enough data, I can recreate her. I can bring her back to life. And I'm willing to do whatever it takes to make that happen."

Noah stepped forward, his fists clenched. "You're insane. You're ruining lives, turning people into monsters, just to bring back your daughter. That's not right."

Principal Parker's expression hardened. "You don't understand. You don't know what it's like to lose someone you love. But soon... very soon... you will."

With a wave of his hand, the screens behind him went dark, and the room was filled with an eerie, pulsating light. The ground beneath their feet began to shift, and the walls started to close in.

"It's time to play," Principal Parker's said, his voice echoing as the room transformed into a twisted version of the school they once knew. "Welcome to Elysium."

This is just the beginning of the story, but it sets the stage for the horror and mystery that will unfold. The group will have to navigate the twisted world of Elysium, uncover the secrets behind obsession, and find a Principal Parker's way to stop the game before it's too late. Along the way, they'll discover that the line between reality and the game is thinner than they ever imagined, and that the true horror may not be the monsters they're fighting— but the darkness within themselves......

Two~

The Haunted Town

PROLOGUE

This story is not just about survival…It's about what happens when the line between entertainment and terror disappears…It's about the things that lurk in the places we're not meant to find…

And most of all—

It's about the price of keeping a promise…By the time you finish reading, you'll understand why some dares should never be made…..And why some towns stay empty for a reason…

There are places in this world that don't follow the rules. Places where the air is too still, where the shadows don't move right, where something older than logic waits in the dark…Lena and Kai walked into one of those places…And whatever came out…Well.

That's the real question, isn't it?…So before you turn the page, ask yourself:

Do you really believe in skinwalkers?

Because by the end of this story—You will.

THE HAUNTED TOWN

Once upon a time, in the bustling city of Los Angeles, there lived a girl named Lena and a boy named Kai.. They were the best of friends and had become famous influencers on social media platforms like YouTube and TikTok...

The world knew them as the unstoppable duo—Lena and Kai with their reckless charm... Best friends since childhood, they built an empire on laughter, and the kind of dares that made their followers hit *subscribe* faster than they could blink...

Whether it was cliff diving in Bali, exploring cursed temples at midnight, or breaking gaming records live on stream, they never shied away from a challenge..

Their channel, "Lena & Kai Adventures," was known for its thrilling travel vlogs and gaming content. Millions of people tuned in every day to watch their videos, and their popularity was skyrocketing...

One evening, as they were live-streaming a gaming session, Lena, made a bold promise to their viewers...

"If we hit 5 million followers," she declared, "I'll dye my hair blue, and we'll spend two weeks in the most haunted town in the world!"

 Kai, always the more cautious one, rolled his eyes but couldn't help laughing at Lena's antics. "Deal!" he agreed, knowing that their fans would love the challenge...

A month later, their channel hit 5 million followers.. To celebrate, they recorded a video where Lena dyed her hair a vibrant shade of blue, much to the delight of their fans...

True to their word, they announced that they would be traveling to a remote, infamous haunted town in China known as "The Empty Mound."

The town was shrouded in mystery and had a terrifying reputation for being overrun by supernatural occurrences and unexplained disappearances... The locals avoided it, and even the bravest adventurers dared not step foot there..

The town had a dozen names, each more ominous than the last. *The Place of Vanished Voices.. The Town That Eats Travelers.* Locals refused to speak of it.. Maps pretended it didn't exist...

A forsaken town in China, whispered about in hushed tones—a place where people vanished, where shadows moved on their own, and where something *not quite human* was said to lurk...

They promised their fans two weeks of exploration, thrills, and the ultimate test of courage...

Excited and a bit nervous, Mia and Ethan packed their bags, loaded up their camera equipment, and set off on their journey. They documented every moment, from the long flights to the dense Chinese forests that led to The forsaken town...

 As they approached the town, they couldn't help but feel a eerie chill in the air.. The town was desolate, with crumbling buildings, overgrown streets, and an unsettling silence that seemed to follow them wherever they went...

At first, Lena and Kai were in high spirits, exploring the town and making light of its spooky reputation. They recorded their adventures, laughing and joking as they wandered through the abandoned streets...

The town was empty.. *Too* empty. Doors hung ajar, belongings were left behind as if people had fled mid-meal, and the air itself felt... *wrong*. At first, they laughed it off, filming their usual antics, teasing each other about jump scares that never came...

 But as the days passed, they began to notice strange signs of life— They found faint claw marks on the walls, strange symbols etched into the ground, and an occasional, unsettling growl echoing in the distance...

Then the *real* horrors began.

Something was watching them. Hunting them. A creature that is a—part human, part beast, with a hunger for flesh and a taste for suffering... Every night brought new terrors..

 Every shadow hid a new nightmare.. Wounded, exhausted, and fighting for their lives, Lena and Kai had to do the impossible: *survive*..

what they found was worse than any ghost story...

One night, while reviewing their footage, they saw something that made their blood run cold... A shadowy, human-animal-like creature darted across the screen... It was tall, with glowing red eyes, razor-sharp claws, and movements that were fast...

They tried to brush it off as a prank or a trick of the light, but deep down, they knew something was wrong...

The following day, they decided to investigate further... They set up cameras around the town and equipped themselves with whatever they could find—sticks, rocks, and even a small first-aid kit...

As night fell, they huddled together in an abandoned house, their hearts pounding with anticipation and fear... They knew they were taking a huge risk, but they couldn't back down now...

Suddenly, a loud crash echoed through the house... The creature had found them...

For the next two weeks, Lena and Kai fought for survival... The creature, which they later learned was known as "The Devourer"...

It hunted them day and night, its claws tearing through walls and its eyes glowing ominously in the dark... Lena and Kai were forced to use their wits, their knowledge of the town's layout, and every trick in the book to evade The Devourer...

They suffered injuries—deep cuts, broken bones, and bruises that ached with every step... But they knew they couldn't give up... They leaned on each other, using their friendship as a source of strength..

Lena kept their spirits high, while Kai, with his quick thinking, devised plans to outsmart their predator...

They set traps using the town's old machinery, created decoys to distract The Devourer, and even used their social media equipment to their advantage, broadcasting their location to throw it off their trail....

Despite the horrors they faced, Lena and Kai found moments of beauty in the town... They discovered hidden gardens, ancient temples, and mysterious artifacts that told the story of The Forsaken Town's dark past...

 They realized that the town wasn't just a place of fear but also a place of history and secrets waiting to be uncovered...

As the days turned into weeks,Lena and Kai grew more determined to escape...

They knew The Devourer was a creature of habit, and they used that to their advantage... They tracked its movements, studied its patterns, and finally discovered its weakness: a rare mineral found only in the town's depths...

The town was a graveyard of half-lived lives...

Dinner tables set for meals never eaten. Beds unmade, as if the occupants had vanished mid-dream... Toys left in the dust, untouched for years...

And the silence...

No birds. No insects..

Just the crunch of their footsteps and the slow, creeping realization that they were not alone..

It was watching them. Hunting them. A creature that is—part human, part beast, with a hunger for flesh and a taste for suffering..

Every night brought new terror..

Every shadow hid a new nightmare...

Wounded, exhausted, and fighting for their lives, Lena and Kai had to do the impossible: *survive..*

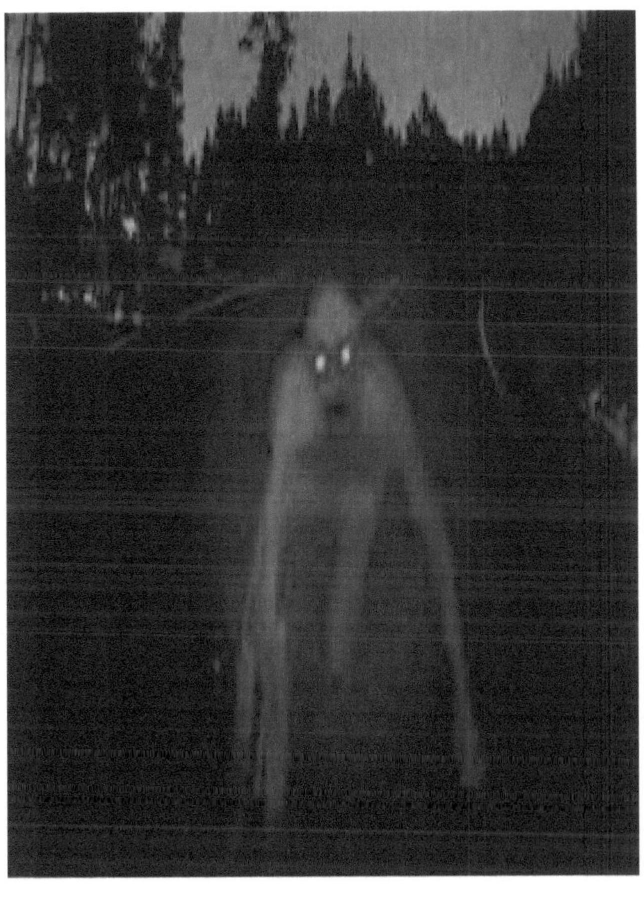

Armed with this knowledge, they devised a final plan...

They lured The Devourer into a trap, using the mineral to keep it at bay while they made a run for the edge of town...

The creature roared in fury as they fled, its claws swiping at the air mere inches from their backs. But Mia and Ethan didn't look back... They ran with every ounce of strength they had, their hearts pounding in their chests, until they finally reached the safety of their car...

As they drove away from The forsaken town, they looked back at the town with a mix of relief..

They had survived against all odds, but the experience had left them changed... They were no longer just influencers chasing likes and views; they were two people who had faced true horror and emerged stronger because of it.....

When they finally returned to Los Angeles, they uploaded their final video from The forsaken town... The footage of their adventure went viral, and their channel gained even more followers...

But Lena and Kai knew that the real prize wasn't the fame or the views—it was

the unbreakable bond they had forged in
the face of danger...

Lena and Kai were greeted with
messages, comments, and notifications
as their final video from the haunted
town went viral...

 The video showed their bravery, their
fear, and their unwavering friendship,
resonating with millions of viewers who
had followed their journey...

The video opened with a shaky shot of the
town's entrance, the camera panning over
the dilapidated buildings and the eerie
mist that hung in the air..

 Lena's voice, filled with a mix of
excitement and, narrated their plan..
They had arrived at The forsaken town at
dusk, the perfect time to set up their
cameras and start their exploration...

 As the night deepened, the atmosphere
grew more tense, and the sounds of their
breathing and footsteps echoed through
the deserted streets...

They visited the town's most notorious
sites, including the abandoned temple
where the legend of The Devourer began...

The temple was a dark, foreboding structure, its walls covered in ancient, cryptic symbols. As they explored, the air grew colder, and the faint sound of whispers seemed to follow them...

Kai , tried to explain the phenomena away, but even he couldn't deny the chill that ran down his spine...

The climax of the video came when they encountered The Devourer itself...

 The creature, a shadowy figure with glowing red eyes, emerged from the darkness, its presence sending a wave of terror through them..

 Lena, quick on her feet, remembered the mineral they had brought to ward off the entity... They used it to create a barrier, giving them just enough time to run...

The video cut to the intense chase scene, with Lena and Kai sprinting through the town, their hearts pounding, and the creature's roars echoing behind them...

The camera shook as they ran, the fear palpable in their voices... Finally, they reached their car and sped away, the creature visible in the rear-view mirror until it disappeared into the mist...

The video ended with Lena and Kai sitting in the car, catching their breath and reflecting on what they had just experienced... They shared a look of mutual understanding, knowing that this adventure had changed them in ways they couldn't yet fully grasp...

Back in Los Angeles, they uploaded the video to their channel, and it quickly gained millions of views.. Comments poured in, praising their bravery and the authenticity of their content...

But more than the views, they were touched by the messages of support and admiration from their followers, who saw in them a reflection of their own courage and friendship...

Lena and Kai decided to take a break from their usual daredevil activities...

They realized that while their adventures brought them fame and excitement, the true value lay in the experiences and the bond they shared...

They started a new series on their channel, focusing on more personal and meaningful content, sharing their thoughts on life, their dreams, and the lessons they had learned from their journey...

Their fans loved the new direction, and the channel continued to grow, but this time, it was with a deeper sense of purpose..

 Lena and Kai had found a new balance, one that allowed them to continue to inspire and entertain their followers while staying true to themselves...

As they looked back on their journey, they knew that the real treasure was the unbreakable bond they had forged in the face of danger...

The forsaken town had tested them, but it had also brought them closer together, proving that sometimes, the greatest adventures are the ones that change you for the better...

Lena and Kai sat in their cozy living room, the glow of the setting sun casting long shadows across the walls adorned with maps and mementos from their past adventures...

 The air was thick with the scent of old books and the faint hum of their computers as they edited their latest video. It had been a few weeks since their escapade at The forsaken town, and the buzz around their channel was still electric..

Fans praised their newfound depth, and their subscriber count continued to increase... Yet, as they sipped their tea, there was an unspoken restlessness between them...

Lena, sighed and leaned back in her chair. "Do you ever feel like we're just going through the motions, Kai? I mean, the adventures are thrilling, but is this all?"

Kai, typically the optimist, looked up from his laptop, his brow furrowed. "You're not having second thoughts, are you? We've built something incredible here..."

Lena shook her head. "No, it's not that. It's just... sometimes I wonder if there's more to this than just views and likes. We started this to challenge ourselves, to push beyond the ordinary. But now, it feels like we're stuck in a loop..."

Kai closed his laptop, the click echoing in the silence...

"Maybe we need a new challenge, something that really pushes us. Something that reminds us why we started this in the first place..."

A knock interrupted their conversation... It was their mailman, holding a dusty, old-fashioned envelope with their name Ruby on It...

"I wonder what it it.." said Lena looking curious...

Inside was a single map, detailing a path through a dense jungle to a location marked only with an 'X'... A note attached read: "For those who seek the truth, follow the path to the Heart of the Ruby Jungle..."

Lena's eyes sparkled as she handed the map to Kai. "Looks like our next adventure just found us..."

And so, they set off, leaving behind the comforts of home for the vibrant expanse of the jungle....

 The air was thick with humidity, and the sounds of wildlife surrounded them as they trekked through the dense forest... The map led them to a hidden entrance, guarded by ancient stones covered in moss and symbols of a long-lost civilization...

As they ventured deeper, the jungle revealed its secrets—hidden waterfalls, ancient ruins, and puzzles that tested their wit... They encountered obstacles:

raging rivers, and even a swarm of angry bees that sent them scrambling..

 But through it all, their bond strengthened... They relied on each other's strengths—Lena's sharp mind and Kai's fearless spirit—navigating each challenge side by side...

The journey was not without its tense moments... In one harrowing instance, Lena found herself trapped in a crumbling temple, the walls closing in as the structure began to collapse...

 Kai, without hesitation, rushed back, his heart pounding in his chest.. Together, they solved the final puzzle—a lock mechanism that required perfect timing— and escaped just as the temple caved in behind them...

They stood outside, catching their breath, the dust settling around them... Lena turned to Kai, her eyes shining with gratitude...

"You saved me back there... I don't know what I'd do without you."

Kai smiled, clapping her on the back... "You'll never have to find out."

Finally, they reached the Heart of the Ruby Jungle—a massive stone statue in the center of a clearing, its base surrounded by a pond of crystal-clear water... The statue depicted two figures standing together, their hands clasped in unity...

Beneath it was an inscription: "The greatest treasure lies not in riches, but in the bonds forged along the way..."

Lena and Kai sat at the edge of the pond, reflecting on their journey... They realized that their adventures, while thrilling, were merely a backdrop for the true treasure—the unbreakable bond they shared...

They had grown, both as individuals and as a team, their experiences shaping them into more resilient, compassionate people...

As they prepared to leave, they documented their findings, sharing their thoughts with their audience... They spoke of growth, of friendship, and the true meaning of adventure...

Their video ended with them standing before the statue, waving to the camera, ready to take on whatever came next..

Their fans loved it, but more importantly, Lena and Kai knew they had found their balance..

 They were no longer just thrill-seekers; they were storytellers, sharing not just their adventures, but the lessons they learned along the way...

And as they made their way back home, they both knew that no matter where their next adventure led, they would face it together, side by side, as the unstoppable duo the world had come to adore and learn...

THE LAST WORDS :

"You're still here?
Then you've seen it all..

The shape that *wasn't human*...

They warned us... They dared us to believe...

And now?

Look outside your window..

The air is too still, isn't it?

You shouldn't have watched...

THE END?

— THEY' RE STILL WATCHING. —

THE LAST PAGE: BREAKING NEWS

MISSING PERSONS CASE..
LENA RIVERA & KAI MONTES
LAST SEEN:NEAR RUBY JUNGLE OUTSKIRTS
STATUS: ACTIVE INVESTIGATION

Police's Report:
"Subjects were last seen exiting the forest outskirts at approximately 11:47 PM on October 31st. Vehicle found abandoned at scene, keys still in.. Personal belongings, including phones and wallets, recovered intact.. No signs of struggle.. No footprints leading away from the site.."

Family Statement:
"They were just teens having fun... Their last video... it looked like they made it out.. But they never came home.."

LAST KNOWN FOOTAGE (ARCHIVED):
The video is cheerful.. Too cheerful.. Lena laughs as Kai high-fives the camera, both breathless, leaves in their hair.. "We did it, guys! Jungle—one, Us—zero!" The frame flickers.. For 0.3 seconds, the reflection in Kai's pupils isn't the trees behind them. It's a shape.. Standing too close. Smiling...

The video ends with Lena's voice, soft but clear: *"Promise you won't forget us?"*

UPDATE: As of [CURRENT DATE], all searches have been suspended. No leads. No traces…

FINAL NOTE FROM INVESTIGATOR:
"Sometimes, people don't want to be found.
And sometimes…
They're not the ones hiding.."

— DON'T TURN AROUND. —

Three~

The Secret

PROLOGUE

Lara Carter transfers to Ashwood High, she expects the usual drama—cliques, homework, maybe a rival. What she doesn't expect is Sarah Grayson: the flawless, brilliant topper who rules the school with a smile… and a knife…

After students linked to Sarah start disappearing, Lara digs deeper—uncovering a labyrinth of horrors beneath the school. But the closer she gets to the truth, the more Sarah tightens her grip. Because in Ashwood, the brightest stars cast the darkest shadows… and Lara's next on her list…

A chilling YA thriller about the secrets behind perfection—and the new girl who dared to expose them.

Whispers in the Dark

The incidents escalated. Lara found her locker vandalized with hateful messages. Someone anonymously submitted a plagiarized essay under her name, resulting in a near-failing grade in English. Rumors spread like wildfire, painting her as a liar, a cheat, and a troublemaker. Even some of her friends started to distance themselves, unsure of what to believe.

Lara felt isolated and alone. She couldn't understand why Sarah hated her so much. She was just trying to be herself, to fit in, to make friends. What had she done to deserve this?

She confided in her parents, but they dismissed her concerns as typical high school drama. They told her to ignore Sarah and focus on her studies. But Lara couldn't ignore it. Sarah's actions were affecting her grades, her friendships, and her mental health.

One evening, while researching for a history project in the library, Lara stumbled upon an old article in the school archives about a series of unsolved disappearances that had plagued Ashwood High decades ago. The article described how several students had vanished without a trace, leaving behind no clues. The police had investigated, but the cases had remained cold.

As Lara read the article, she noticed a recurring theme. All of the missing students had been popular, talented, and successful. They had been the "stars" of Ashwood High, the ones who were destined for greatness. And they had all disappeared shortly after reaching the peak of their popularity.

A chill ran down Lara's spine. She couldn't shake the feeling that there was a connection between the disappearances and Sarah. Was it possible that Sarah was somehow involved? Was she responsible for the missing students?

She dismissed the idea as ridiculous. Sarah was a mean girl, but she wasn't a murderer. Or was she?

Driven by a growing sense of unease, Lara decided to investigate. She started by researching Sarah's family history. She learned that Sarah came from a long line of prominent Ashwood residents. Her family had been involved in local politics, business, and philanthropy for generations. They were respected and admired by the community.

But Lara also discovered a dark secret in Sarah's family history. Decades ago, Sarah's great-aunt had been accused of murdering her rival in a local beauty pageant. The case had been circumstantial, and the great-aunt had been acquitted, but the scandal had haunted the family for years.

Could Sarah be following in her great-aunt's footsteps? Was she continuing a legacy of violence and jealousy?

Lara knew she needed more evidence. She decided to focus her investigation on Sarah's activities. She started observing her, watching her interactions with others, and trying to piece together her secrets.

The Mask Slips

Lara started spending more time at school, observing Sarah. She noticed that Sarah had a tight-knit group of friends who seemed completely devoted to her. They followed her every word, and protected her from any perceived threats. They were like a loyal pack, ready to defend their leader at any cost.

One of Sarah's closest friends was a girl named Madison. Madison was beautiful and popular, but she always seemed nervous and anxious. She often looked at Sarah with a mixture of admiration and fear.

Lara suspected that Madison knew something about Sarah's secrets. She decided to try and befriend her, hoping to glean some information.

She started by complimenting Madison on her clothes, her hair, and her academic achievements. She invited her to join her and her friends for lunch, and she offered to help her with her homework.

At first, Madison was wary. She seemed suspicious of Lara's motives. But as Lara continued to be friendly and supportive, Madison started to open up.

She confided in Lara about her insecurities, her fears, and her dreams.

One day, Lara decided to broach the subject of Sarah. "You and Sarah seem really close," Lara said casually. "How long have you known each other?"

Madison hesitated, her eyes darting around nervously. "We've been friends since kindergarten," she said. "Our families are really close."

"Sarah seems like a really strong person," Lara said, probing gently. "She's so confident and successful."

Madison's expression darkened. "She is," she said quietly. "But she can also be...intense. She expects a lot from her friends. She doesn't like to be challenged or questioned."

"Has she ever...hurt anyone?" Lara asked, holding her breath.

Madison's eyes widened in alarm. "What do you mean?" she stammered.

"I just mean...has she ever done anything that made you uncomfortable?" Lara said, trying to backpedal.

Madison was silent for a long moment. Then, she leaned closer to Lara and whispered, "I can't talk about it. Sarah would kill me."

Lara felt a surge of adrenaline. Madison knew something. She was afraid of Sarah.

"I won't tell anyone," Lara said, her voice urgent. "You can trust me. I think Sarah is dangerous. I think she's hiding something."

Madison looked at Lara, her eyes filled with fear and desperation. "I...I can't," she said. "I'm sorry. I have to go."

Madison stood up and hurried away, leaving Lara alone with her suspicions. Lara's instincts told her that she was getting closer to the truth. Sarah was hiding something, and Madison knew what it was.

Later that day, Lara witnessed an incident that confirmed her worst fears. She was walking past the school gym when she heard a commotion inside. She peeked through the window and saw Sarah yelling at another student, a shy, awkward boy named Kevin.

Kevin had accidentally bumped into Sarah in the hallway, spilling her coffee. Sarah was furious. She berated him, insulted him, and threatened to ruin his life.

"You're a worthless piece of trash," Sarah screamed at Kevin. "You're lucky I don't have you expelled."

Kevin was trembling with fear. He apologized profusely, but Sarah wouldn't let up. She continued to verbally abuse him, pushing him to the brink of tears.

Lara couldn't stand to watch any longer. She burst into the gym and confronted Sarah.

"Leave him alone, Sarah," Lara said, her voice trembling with anger. "You're being cruel and unfair."

Sarah turned to Lara, her eyes

fuming "Stay out of this, Lara," she hissed. "This is none of your business."

"It is my business," Lara said, standing her ground. "You can't just bully people like this. It's wrong."

Sarah glared at Lara, her face contorted with rage. "You think you're so righteous, don't you?" she said. "You think you're better than everyone else."

"I don't think I'm better than anyone," Lara said. "I just think you're being a horrible person."

Sarah lunged at Lara, shoving her against the wall. "You're going to regret this," she said. "You're going to regret ever crossing me."

Before Sarah could do anything else, a teacher walked into the gym. Sarah immediately composed herself, putting on a sweet, innocent smile.

"Everything's fine, Mr. Thompson," Sarah said smoothly. "Lara and I were just having a friendly chat."

Mr. Thompson looked at Lara skeptically. "Is that true, Lara?" he asked.

Lara hesitated. She knew that if she told the truth, Sarah would retaliate. But she couldn't lie.

"No," Lara said, her voice barely a whisper. "It's not true. Sarah was bullying Kevin. She was threatening him."

Mr.Thompson frowned. He knew that Sarah was a difficult student, but he had never seen her act like this before.

"Sarah, is this true?" Mr.Thompson asked sternly.

Sarah's facade finally cracked. Her eyes flashed with anger, and her face turned red.

"It's not true," she spat. "Lara is lying. She's trying to make me look bad."

Mr.Thompson looked from Lara to Sarah, unsure of who to believe. He decided to take them both to the principal's office to sort out the situation.

Terror

The principal, Mr. Thompson, listened to both sides of the story. He was a seasoned educator, but he seemed hesitant to believe Lara's accusations against Sarah. Sarah was, after all, a model student, a leader, and a favorite of many teachers. Lara, on the other hand, was the new girl, still trying to find her footing.

"I find it hard to believe that Sarah would act in such a way," Mr. Thompson said, his voice measured. "She has always been a responsible and respectful student."

"But it's true," Lara insisted. "I saw it with my own eyes. She was bullying Kevin. She was threatening him."

Mr. Thompson sighed. "Well, I'll speak to Kevin and get his side of the story. In the meantime, I want you both to stay away from each other. No more confrontations, no more accusations. Is that clear?"

Lara and Sarah nodded in agreement. As they left the principal's office, Sarah shot Lara a venomous look.

"You haven't seen the last of me," she hissed. "This isn't over."

Lara knew that Sarah was right. This was far from over. In fact, it was just the beginning.

That night, Lara couldn't sleep. She tossed and turned in her bed, replaying the events of the day in her mind.

She was convinced that Sarah was dangerous, but she didn't know how to prove it. She needed more evidence. She needed to find something that would expose Sarah's true nature.

She remembered the unsolved disappearances that she had read about in the school archives. She wondered if there was a connection between those cases and Sarah. She decided to do some more research.

The next day, Lara returned to the library. She spent hours poring over old newspapers, yearbooks, and school records. She was looking for any clues that might link Sarah to the missing students.

As she digged deeper into the archives, she started to notice some disturbing patterns. All of the missing students had been rivals of Sarah in some way. They had challenged her academically, athletically, or socially. They had threatened her position as the "star" of Ashwood High.

And they had all disappeared shortly after crossing paths with Sarah.

Lara felt a chill run down her spine. The evidence was mounting. Sarah was not just a mean girl. She was something far more sinister.

She remembered the old article that had mentioned the series of rooms beneath the school, abandoned during a renovation long ago. People said those rooms were never opened to the public. They thought that the rooms were where the old students were kept

She started searching for the blueprints of the school, hoping to find a map of the underground tunnels. After hours of searching, she finally found what she was looking for. A faded and crumbling blueprint that showed a network of tunnels and rooms beneath the school.

Lara stared at the blueprint in disbelief. The tunnels were far more extensive than she had imagined. They stretched beneath the entire school building, connecting to various classrooms, offices, and storage areas. And in the center of the network, there was a cluster of rooms that were labeled "RESTRICTED ACCESS."

Lara knew that she had to explore those rooms. She had to find out what Sarah was hiding.

That night, after everyone had left, Lara snuck back into the school. She used her knowledge of the building's security system to disable the alarms and gain access to the underground tunnels.

Armed with a flashlight and a map, she ventured into the darkness. The tunnels were cold, damp, and eerily silent. The air was thick with the smell of mold and decay.

As she navigated the labyrinthine passages, she couldn't shake the feeling that she was being watched. She heard strange noises echoing through the tunnels—*scurrying sounds, whispers, and faint moans.*

Finally, she reached the cluster of rooms that were labeled "RESTRICTED ACCESS." The doors were locked , but Lara managed to pry them open using a crowbar that she had found in one of the tunnels.

She stepped inside the first room, her heart pounding in her chest. The room was dark and dusty, filled with cobwebs and debris. As she shined her flashlight around, she saw something that made her blood run cold.

The walls of the room were covered in graffiti. But this wasn't the kind of graffiti that you find in a public restroom. This was something far more disturbing.

The graffiti consisted of names, dates, and cryptic messages written in blood. The names were all the names of the missing students. The dates were the dates of their disappearances. And the messages were chillingly vague:

"She's coming for you."

"You're next."

"There's no escape."

Lara stumbled back in horror. She had found the "rooms of terror." Sarah had been using these rooms to torture and torment her victims.

She stepped into the next room. This room was even more disturbing than the first. It was filled with torture devices—racks, chains, whips, and other implements of pain. The devices were old and rusty, but they were still functional.

Lara realized that Sarah had been using these devices to torture her victims before killing them. She was a sadistic monster.

In the final room, Lara found the most disturbing sight of all. In the center of the room, there was a table. And on the table, there was a body.

The body was that of Madison, Sarah's closest friend. Her eyes were wide with terror, and her mouth was open in a silent scream. She had been tortured to death.

Lara gasped in horror. She realized that Madison had been trying to warn her about Sarah. She had known too much, and Sarah had silenced her.

Lara knew that she was in grave danger. Sarah was a serial killer, and she was her next target.

She had to escape. She had to get out of the school and call the police.

But as she turned to leave, she heard a noise behind her. She whirled around and saw Sarah standing in the doorway, her eyes gleaming with madness.

"Hello, Lara," Sarah said, her voice dripping with venom. "I've been expecting you.

A chill ran down Lara's spine. Was it possible that Sarah's animosity ran deeper than mere high-school rivalry? Could she be hiding something more sinister?

Suddenly, the library door creaked open, and Sarah walked in, her eyes scanning the room until they landed on Lara. A smirk played on her lips as she approached.

"Looking for something, Lara?" she asked, her voice a low, mocking purr.

Lara quickly closed the browser window, trying to hide the article, but it was too late. Sarah had seen it. Her smirk widened, and her eyes gleamed with a strange, unsettling light.

"Interesting choice of reading material," Sarah said, her tone laced with amusement. "Are you trying to dig up the past?"

Lara's heart pounded in her chest. "I... I was just doing research for a project," she stammered, trying to maintain her composure.

"Right," Sarah said, her voice dripping with sarcasm. "And I'm sure you just happened to stumble upon those old articles by accident." She leaned closer, her voice a whisper. "Some things are better left buried, Lara. You wouldn't want to end up like those unfortunate students, would you?"

Lara recoiled, her mind racing. Was Sarah threatening her? Was she hinting at some dark secret connected to the disappearances? She couldn't shake the feeling that she was getting closer to something dangerous, something that Sarah was desperate to keep hidden.

That night, Lara couldn't sleep. She kept replaying Sarah's words in her mind, trying to decipher their meaning. She knew she couldn't let Sarah intimidate her, but she also knew that she had to be careful. Sarah was powerful, and she wouldn't hesitate to use her influence to silence anyone who threatened her.

Driven by a mixture of fear and determination, Lara decided to investigate the disappearances further. She enlisted the help of Sam, the only friend who truly believed her. Together, they started digging into the school archives, searching for clues that might shed light on the mystery.

They discovered old yearbooks, newspaper clippings, and student records, piecing together a timeline of the events. They learned that all of the missing students had been on the verge of uncovering some kind of scandal involving the school administration. Could this be connected to Sarah? Was she protecting someone or something?

As they delved deeper into their investigation, Lara and Sam started to uncover a series of unsettling coincidences. They discovered that each of the missing students had been warned to stop their investigation by an anonymous source. They also found that Sarah's family had a long and influential history at Ashwood High, with generations of alumni holding positions of power in the school administration.

The more they learned, the more convinced Lara became that Sarah was involved in something sinister. She knew she had to find proof, but how could she do that without putting herself in danger?

One afternoon, while searching through an old box of forgotten artifacts in the school's basement, Lara stumbled upon a hidden compartment in a dusty wooden chest. Inside, she found a small, leather-bound diary. The diary belonged to one of the missing students, Sarah Jenkins.

With trembling hands, Lara opened the diary and began to read. Sarah's words painted a vivid picture of a school shrouded in secrets, a place where power and privilege reigned supreme. She wrote about a secret society that controlled the school from the shadows, manipulating events to protect their interests. She also wrote about Sarah's family and their involvement in the society.

As Lara read on, she realized that she had stumbled upon something explosive, something that could expose the truth about the disappearances and bring down the entire power structure at Ashwood High. But she also knew that she was playing a dangerous game. Sarah and her allies wouldn't hesitate to silence her if they found out what she knew.

The diary ended abruptly, with Sarah writing about being followed and feeling like she was in imminent danger. The last entry was dated the day before she disappeared.

Lara closed the diary, her heart pounding in her chest. She had the proof she needed, but she also knew that she was in serious danger. She had to find a way to expose the truth without becoming the next victim.

She looked at Sam, his eyes wide with concern. "We need to be careful," she whispered. "Sarah knows we're getting close. We need to find a way to expose her and the society before they have a chance to silence us."

The battle for truth and justice had begun. Lara knew that she was facing a formidable enemy, but she was determined to fight for her voice, her identity, and the memory of those who had been silenced before her. Ashwood High held secrets, and Lara was ready to bring them into the light. She just had to survive long enough to do it.

The leather-bound diary felt heavy in Lara's hands, its pages yellowed with age but the ink still dark—as if Sarah Jenkins' fear had been preserved in time.

Sam leaned closer, his breath uneven. *"This is it, isn't it? Proof that Sarah's family is connected to the disappearances."*

Lara nodded, tracing Sarah's frantic handwriting. *"She knew too much. And now..."* Her voice caught as she flipped to the last entry.

LARA'S FINAL WORDS

(scrawled in shaky script):

"They're watching me. The Society knows I've seen their records.

Sarah came to my house last night—just stood there, smiling in the dark. She said, 'Some stories aren't meant to be told.' If I go missing, it's not an accident.

IT'S THEM."

A floorboard creaked upstairs.

Lara and Sam froze.

Sam whispered, *"We're not alone."*

The Hunt Begins

Sarah's voice slithered through the basement door. *"Lara? I know you're down there."*

Lara's blood turned to ice. She shoved the diary into her backpack and grabbed Sam's arm. *"Back exit—now."*

They sprinted past rusted lockers, Sarah's laughter echoing behind them. *"Running just makes it more fun!"*

That night, Lara pored over the diary in her bedroom, decoding Sarah's notes:

> The Ashwood Legacy Society: A secret group of alumni (including Sarah's parents) who controlled the school's funding, staff, and— most chillingly—its *secrets*..

> The "Pruning": Their term for removing "threats"—students who dug too deep.

> The Underground Rooms: Not just for torture... but for *disposal.*

A knock at her window made her jump.

Maya stood outside, her face pale. *"Lara, you need to go. Sarah's coming for you. Tonight."*

Lara barely had time to hide the diary before her bedroom door burst open.

Sarah stood there, her usual polished demeanor gone. Her eyes were wild, her smile unhinged...

"Did you really think you could expose us?" She held up Lara's phone—*her evidence photos deleted.*

Lara backed against the wall. *"The police already know. Sam has copies—"*

Sarah laughed. *"Sam's loyalty... is negotiable."* She stepped closer, a glint of metal in her hand. *"But you? You're irreplaceable."*

The Final Revelation

As Sarah lunged, Lara ducked, grabbing the fireplace poker.

Sarah sneered. *"You're just like Sarah. And Madison. And all the others who thought they could win."*

Lara swung. *"No. I'm the one who ends you."*

To Be Continued....

"You Thought This Was Over?"

The police found Sarah's body, of course. Cold.
Still. Perfect, even in death. They closed the case.
The town sighed in relief. The whispers about
"that unstable honor student" faded.

But you and I? We know better.

Did you really think it ended there? That the
Ashwood Legacy Society just... disappeared?
Look closer. That new teacher watching you a little
too intently? The principal's too-polished smile?
The way your locker door creaks open at night
when no one's there?

Sarah's diary is still missing. Pages torn out.
Names scratched away.

Sleep well, reader...

THE END...

(...knock knock)

FOUR~

Behind the Honors

PROLOGUE

SHORT STORY

The first time I noticed something was wrong, it was small—a pencil missing from my desk, a whisper as I walked past the girls' bathroom... Then came the failing grade on an exam I *knew* I'd aced. The teachers sighed, shaking their heads... *"You must have misremembered, Aria..."*

But I didn't...

Nyra—top of the class, darling of the faculty, the girl with the perfect smile—was behind it... I just didn't know yet....

This isn't just a story about bullying... It's about what happens when the quiet girl finally fights back...

The world often sees only what is on the surface.... It rarely notices the currents beneath it..

 The quiet observers who wait, who plan, and who strike when least expected...

This is the story of a girl who was once the target of sabotage, and betrayal... But she was not weak... She was just... waiting...!!

Hazel was a girl who had always been bullied by her silence.. In a school where the loudest voices often dominated, Hazel preferred to keep to herself...

She was a shy, studious girl who had never been one to seek the spotlight.. But her quietness made her an easy target for those who thrived on power and control...

At the prestigious Rosewood Law Academy , Hazel was constantly bullied by the school's top student, Nyra, and a few teachers who seemed to take pleasure in her misery..

 Nyra was the student of perfection, or so it seemed.. She was the top scorer, the captain of the debate team, and the favorite of the teachers...

But beneath her polished exterior, Nyra was a master manipulator who used her influence to sabotage Hazel at every turn..

The teachers, particularly ,Ms.Vivian and Mr.Eldrin, were a part in Nyra's schemes.. They would often turn a blind eye to Nyra's behavior, sometimes even actively contributing to Hazel's plans...

They saw Hazel as a threat, a potential rival to Nyra's dominance.. And so, they worked together to ensure that Hazel never had a chance to succeed..

But Hazel was not weak.. She was just biding her time, waiting for the right moment to strike back..

She knew that patience was a virtue, and she was determined to prove that even the quietest of voices could make the loudest impact..

Hazel's days were filled with the constant dread of what Nyra and the teachers might do next.. She was isolated, with no friends to turn to..

Her classmates either feared Nyra too much to stand up for her or simply didn't care.. Hazel refused to let it break her..

One day, Nyra took her bullying too far.. She confronted Hazel in the hallway, taunting her about her grades and her appearance..

"Why don't you just drop out?" Nyra sneered.. "No one wants you here.."

Hazel didn't respond.. She just stood there, her eyes fixed on the floor, as Nyra's words cut deep.. But inside, she was hurt.. She knew that Nyra's words were not just random insults; they were part of a larger plan to break her spirit..

That night, Hazel sat in her small room, staring at the wall as tears streamed down her face.. She felt powerless, but she knew she couldn't give up..

She had to fight back, no matter how difficult it seemed..

Weeks turned into months, and Hazel continued to endure the endless bullying.. But she was not just enduring; she was observing..

She noticed the way Nyra and the teachers seemed to communicate in hushed tones, the way they would often disappear into the school's old wing during lunch breaks..

One day, Hazel decided to follow them.. She kept a safe distance, her heart pounding in her chest as she watched Nyra and Ms. Vivian slip into a door hidden behind a row of lockers..

The door was old and rusted, with a sign that read "Storage Room — Authorized Persons Only.."

Hazel waited until they were inside before she approached the door.. She pressed her ear against it, and what she heard made her blood run cold..

"We need to make sure she doesn't pass the final exams," Ms.Vivian said.. "If she does, she might become a threat.."

"Don't worry, I've already taken care of it," Nyra replied.. "Her papers have been tampered with.. She won't even know what hit her..."

Hazel's eyes widened as she realized the extent of their sabotage.. They were not just bullying her; they were trying to ruin her future...

 But she didn't have time to process this information.. She heard footsteps coming from inside the room and quickly retreated, her mind racing with thoughts of what she had just overheard...

Hazel knew she had to act fast.. She couldn't let Nyra and the teachers get away with what they were doing..

But she also knew that she couldn't confront them directly—not yet.. So, she decided to gather evidence..

Over the next few weeks, Hazel kept a close eye on Nyra and the teachers..

She followed them whenever they went into the old wing, always staying out of sight..

She recorded their conversations, took pictures of the documents they handled, and even managed to sneak into the storage room one night to gather physical evidence...

What she found was shocking..

There were files on her, detailing every aspect of her life..

There were notes on how to sabotage her, how to make her look bad in front of the other students, and how to ensure she failed her exams..

Hazel felt a wave of anger wash over her, but she didn't let it consume her..

She knew that anger would cloud her judgment, and she needed to stay focused...

She began to collect the evidence , creating a detailed timeline of Nyra and the teachers' schemes...

She knew that when the time was right, she would expose them for who they truly were..

The day of the final exams arrived, and Hazel was ready... She had spent months preparing for this moment, and she was not going to let anyone take it away from her...

As she sat in the exam hall, she noticed Nyra glance at her with a smug look on her face.. Hazel ignored her, focusing on her paper instead...

But as she began to answer the questions, she realized that something was off... The questions were nothing like what she had studied...

They were difficult, almost impossible, and she knew that she wasn't the only one struggling..

She glanced around the room and saw that the other students were equally confused...

That's when it hit her—Nyra and the teachers had tampered with the exam papers...

They had made sure that the questions were impossible to answer, ensuring that Hazel would fail...

But Hazel was not going to let that happen...
She had a plan..

She waited until the exam was over before she made her move...

As the students filed out of the hall, Hazel approached the principal's office...

She had an appointment scheduled, and she was ready to expose everything...

The principal looked up as Hazel entered his office.. "Can I help you, Hazel?" he asked, his voice cold..

"Yes, sir," Hazel replied, her voice steady.. "I have something important to share with you.."

She placed a folder on his desk, filled with all the evidence she had gathered over the past few months..

The principal opened it, and his expression changed from curiosity to shock as he flipped through the pages...

"This... this is serious," he stuttered.. "Where did you get this?"

"I gathered it myself," Hazel said.. "Nyra and the teachers have been sabotaging me for months...

They tampered with my exam papers, spread rumors about me, and even tried to isolate me from my classmates... They thought I was weak, but they were wrong..."

The principal looked at her with a mixture of guilt and admiration.. "I had no idea," he said..

"I'm sorry, Hazel... This should have never happened..

I'll make sure that Nyra and the teachers involved are held accountable for their actions..."

Hazel nodded, her heart heavy with emotion...

"Thank you, sir. But I want more than just accountability.. I want justice.."

The weeks that followed were a whirlwind of change at Rosewood Law Academy.. The principal, true to his word, launched a thorough investigation into the evidence Hazel had provided...

Nyra and the teachers involved were called into questioning, and the truth began to unravel...

The school community was shocked as the details of the sabotage and bullying surfaced..

Nyra, once the epitome of perfection, was revealed to be a mastermind of manipulation, and the teachers who had supported her were exposed for their complicity...

The fallout was immediate... Nyra was expelled, and the teachers involved were fired...

The principal issued a public apology to Hazel and the school community, promising to create a safer and more inclusive environment for all students...

 Measures were put in place to prevent such abuse of power in the future, and a new system of accountability was implemented to protect students like Hazel...

But for Hazel, the real victory was not in seeing her tormentors punished, though that brought her a sense of closure..

 It was in the way her courage inspired others...

Students who had once stood by in silence began to speak up, sharing their own stories of struggle and resilience...

The school, once dominated by fear and intimidation, began to transform into a place of unity and support...

she later graduated as a top student of law and certainly beat the topper Nyra and made an awesome change as the most confident, most intelligent student...

Hazel's victory was not just personal; it was a revolution... The school that had once thrived on fear and manipulation was now a place of hope and unity...

Students who had suffered in silence found the courage to speak up, inspired by Hazel's bravery...

The teachers who had once turned a blind eye to injustice were now held to a higher standard, and the school administration worked tirelessly to create a fair and supportive environment. ..

For Hazel, however, this was only the beginning... She had faced her tormentors and exposed their lies, but she knew that her true purpose lay beyond the walls of Rosewood Law Academy...

 She had always been a studious girl, but her experiences had given her a newfound determination...

She decided to pursue a career in law, determined to fight for justice and protect others from suffering the same fate she had endured...

Years passed, and Hazel's hard work paid off... She earned a scholarship to one of the most prestigious law schools in the country, where she quickly made a name for herself as a brilliant and fearless student..

 Her classmates admired her intellect, and her professors praised her passion for justice.. But there was one person who did not take kindly to Hazel's rise: Nyra, the law school's top student and a fierce rival who had always been used to being the best.. and also the one who is being hated by all now..

Nyra was everything Hazel was not—loud, arrogant, and ruthless... She saw Hazel as a threat to her dominance and began to undermine her at every turn..

But Hazel was not the same shy girl she had once been... She had grown into a confident, intelligent, and determined woman, and she was not about to let Nyra stand in her way again...

One day, the two were paired together for a high-stakes moot court competition, a simulation of a courtroom trial where students argued cases in front of real judges...

Nyra was thrilled at the opportunity to outshine Hazel, but she soon realized that she had underestimated her opponent... Hazel's arguments were flawless, her delivery commanding...

By the end of the competition, it was clear to everyone in the courtroom that Hazel was the superior lawyer...

Nyra was furious, but Hazel just smiled,... She had proven once again that silence was not weakness, and that even the quietest voices could make the loudest impact...

Years later, Hazel stood in a packed courtroom, her voice ringing out as she defended a young girl who had been bullied and silenced, just as she had once been...

The defendant, a powerful figure who had thought himself above the law, sat trembling in the dock, knowing that he had met his match...

"Your Honor, the evidence is clear," Hazel said, her voice steady and firm... "The defendant has abused his power and destroyed lives..

 But today, we say enough.. Today, we stand up for the voiceless, for the silent, and for the ones who have been wronged... Justice will be served.."

The courtroom erupted in silence as the judge banged his gavel, saying 'Guilty'... Hazel had won the case, but more importantly, she had won justice for her client...

As she walked out of the courtroom, she felt a sense of pride and fulfillment... She had come a long way from the shy, silenced girl she once was...

She had become a force of change, a protector of the vulnerable, and a beacon of hope for those who had lost their voice...

And so, Hazel's story became a legend, a reminder to the world that even in the darkest moments, there is always the power to rise, to fight, and to make a difference...

 She had once been defined by her silence, but now she was defined by her courage, her intelligence, and her commitment to justice...

Hazel's journey was far from over, but one thing was certain: the quietest voice had become the loudest, and she would never be silenced again...

*"You've read the last page. But the story isn't done with you yet.

Somewhere, in the quiet between your heartbeat and your next breath, something stirs. A whisper you can't quite hear. A shadow that doesn't match the light.

Did you really think these were just stories?

Turn off the light. Close your eyes. Tell yourself it isn't real.

But when the walls start breathing—when the laughter comes from nowhere—when your reflection blinks back a second too slow—

Remember: You were warned...

"The final page turns... but the story never ends..

Remember : *You kept reading when you should have stopped...*
You looked when you should have turned away..
And now... they know your name too.

Sleep tight, reader.
We'll be waiting when you wake...

Or better ...
We'll be waiting when you don't. "

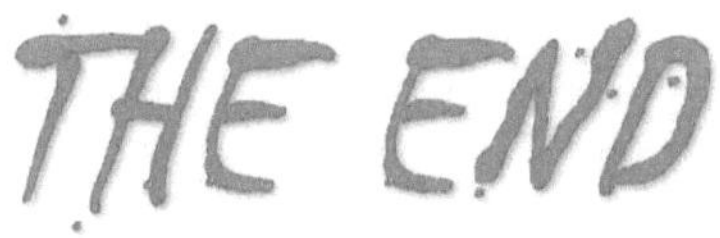